RUBY CAMP

&

TRAVELLING ALONE TOGETHER

Ruby Camp

a Snowy River series

Louise Crisp

travelling alone together

in the footsteps of Edward John Eyre

Miriel Lenore

Spinifex Press Pty Ltd
504 Queensberry Street
North Melbourne, Vic. 3051
Australia
women@spinifexpress.com.au
http://www.spinifexpress.com.au/~women

Edited by Alex Skovron
Typeset in Garamond, Gill Sans and Optima by Claire Warren
Cover design by Nick Stewart – design BITE
Made and printed in Australia by Australian Print Group

National Library of Australia
Cataloguing-in-Publication data:

Crisp, Louise, 1957–   .
  Ruby Camp.

  ISBN 1-875559-83-3

  1. Eyre, Edward John, 1815–1901 – Journeys – Australia – Poetry.
  2. Australia – Description and travel – Poetry. I. Lenore, Miriel.
  Travelling alone together. II. Title. III. Title: Travelling alone
  together.

A821.3

This publication is assisted by the Australia Council, the
Australian Government's arts funding and advisory body.

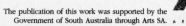

The publication of this work was supported by the
Government of South Australia through Arts SA.

Contents

Ruby Camp

a Snowy River series

Louise Crisp

For Moo

Louise Crisp was born in Omeo, Victoria. She majored in Linguistics, Anthropology and Prehistory at the Australian National University in Canberra. She has worked in various occupations around New Zealand and Australia including firetower person on Mt Nugong in East Gippsland, and deckhand on fishing boats in the Northern Territory and Western Australia.

Her first collection of poetry, *the luminous ocean*, was published in a joint volume with Valery Wilde entitled *In the Half-Light* (Friendly Street Poets, 1988); *pearl & sea fed* (Hazard Press, 1994) was shortlisted in the 1995 NSW Premier's Awards. She lives in East Gippsland with her partner and two daughters.

Acknowledgements

Poems in this collection have previously appeared in *Australian Women's Book Review*, *Hobo*, *Meanjin*, *Poetrix* and *Scripsi*.

My thanks to P. D. Gardiner for permission to quote from his *Gippsland Massacres* in my poem 'karst'. Full details are given in the Notes.

This work was assisted by a Project Grant (Literature) from Arts Victoria, a division of the Department of Arts, Sport and Tourism.

Ruby Camp

Contents

I

Pattern

feltas

1

Snowy River pine & xanthorrhoea
define the warmth gradient
out of the valley
the sun works
its way around the north
face of old boulders
& shale
goes up into steepness
abruptly as a gift should

2

something attracts
your interest. alert
floods through / disappears
the ordinary focuses
on a tin cup near the campfire
he says:
there's nothing out there
as if nothing is
equivalent
to the unvisited

3

everpresent is background noise
you want to put your hands over . . .
but the mind
develops a technique
for silence
like several thousand years
with the *Diamond Sutra*
you notice
that insight has become inseparable
from recognition. like a striking place
you could pull the canoe up to
along a sandbar
on any big bend of the river

thanks George Bell (photographer)

I'm looking for Ruby
along the headwaters
cousin of my great-grandfather
near Paupong in 1905

a skilled horsewoman:
any approach to the Snowy
is rough & steep
and goes direct to the heart

of an early persistent myth
from the region
i.e. post 1890
there is invariably some man

racing between the stringybarks
shouting for a challenge
while Ruby leads her horse
that last little bit to water

stance pattern I
cripple

to be cut open
& crystals inserted
is no escape?

stamp around the fire with the old
body & the new
through smoke

arms & palms extended
to receive via the flat gesture
& lateral for gifts

becoming two carved snakes
& the gleam of skin
twists above my head

karst

the water spins underground
each frill of water is muscle white
& clear
as bone scraping
a song for the dead

> *tumbledown johnny*
> *tumbledown jack*
> *what would we hear*
> *if history were black?*

coming down the gully
the men are unafraid to ride with their faces uncovered
like an article of faith: 'thieves and damned savages'
& a gun under the saddleflaps can make them feel.
the horses trot quietly over hollow ground

> *bones & stones*
> *& bodies that crack*
> *on boulders & blood*
> *it's breaking our back*

J. Macleod writes to A. W. Howitt:
'My brother Norman and I, and seven Omeo blacks,
surrounded them . . . in the Murrindal River just
    below The Pyramids.
. . . I killed a bullock for them and they ate till they
    were sick.'

> *blackness is skin*
> *blackness is terror*
> *black as the sun*
> *when you're held under water*

history diverts underground for 115 years
re-emerges in *The Gap* magazine 1966:
'. . . the aborigines who were feasting on the banks
    of a lagoon
behind The Pyramids. Confronted by the white men
    and all chance
of escape cut off by the steep cliffs of the
    Murrindal River,
the tribe had no chance of escape . . .'

> *worn smooth & hollow*
> *as a cup of bone*
> *the bed of the river*
> *is a river of stone*

the clear water runs around each worn stone
spills into joints & hollows
where the river runs underground
the bodies were thrown

stance pattern II
banish or the Pyramids

the hands listen between the stones
taut as ears

the palms vertical
& arms stretched out straight

turn to the east stone
turn to the west stone

turning opens the space
& strength enters

facing north
your hands cross over your heart

as if out of the act
comes a rich old woman-song

— how could you not say:
the earth mothers me

when I'm banished
abide with me

memory / & the pattern of the stance
restore me over

Murrindal

just upstream
from the Pyramids
the water, the rocks
the aspect
of sun on the limestone bluff
each day denies
the clean washed light
of TV sets
each night
flowing out through the dark
from the 3 houses
in Murrindal valley
& the quiet
of their English country gardens
just north of Buchan.
where Butchers Creek
Slaughterhouse Gully
& Butchers Ridge
mean that locals still joke
when one of them burns
another canoe tree down

birdstones

at the confluence
Buchan/Snowy proffers
a small stone
white & black speckles
a little quail's egg
stone
         or
būlk — the stone
turned away from
the stone of terror
here is the almighty
fear, the swamping fear
a wall of muddy water
smelt and tasted
advances down the breadth
of the river
the overcoming, choking
unable to breathe fear
       the stone guides the fear
to the listener
       the smeller, the taster
              the dead ones
           būlk — the stone
turned away from
I can't say their names:
the dead
or because I never knew them.

I wrap the stone in a bark package:
when it cannot see
I cannot see through it
buried in mud

būlk — power stone (Gunai/Kurnai)

Freestone

with children on our backs & following
behind us
through the snow gums
we round each rocky knob/knoll
                        to bless
the valley
with our expectoring breath
and gasp across to Rams Horn

— follow that hot brumby shit
sign / up the last grassy haul to the summit

        nobody a brave
                    hero
        or rider for Indians

& the one who leaves our names in the book
is neither game nor aware
that south-east across the cliffs
Freestone spur was the route
all those draywheel ancestors
came by into here

crossing / ford I

downstream from Gattamurh
(*the wheels of the Toyota go round & round*)

my baby's head against the sky
I laugh like a blue child
& clouds scuff over
the white-pine ridges

when the moon rises into your face
I see how
you both sleep
in the bright pale light
that bodies make

in a deep pool near camp
the bunyip who lives here
swallows our shadows

sejant

I come into her country
the dingo observes me
seeking a trail across
the river
padding back & forth
then sitting to wait
on a sandbar
the wind does not
disturb her or my smell

having watched this long on the track
a call may do it
or a cry
or someone she slept near
a long time ago

I wait
for the scent of memory
then go /
           lie down by her

unborn

like a stone that bled
two children
have left me

where bird prints
mark the sand
below a cliff

I lay them out
so tiny
just a cluster of cells

I wrapped around
tightly as bodies
inside me

I heap
two small graves
of sand

less than the length
from my hand
to elbow:

a single twig
at the head of each
marking the ascent

quartz

the pink oval stone is my mask
the one possibility of many possibilities.
when a sister is given it
she goes in search of masks
high & low for masks
in foreign countries & beyond
she searches inside her own gizzard
                    taking feathers
from ancient birds she has never seen
sewing them as soft as possible
to brush my skin
with the scent
of possibilities

little stones the size of bird droppings
nestle in the fluff glued for eyes
I have spoken to her many times about it
                    with tail feathers like flags
the mask reaches below
my shoulders
& the pink stone she carries airborne
nestles like a heart
in the song of possibilities

fascination & egg

'smaller at the top
and wider at the bottom
they're egg-shaped'

we tip the kids out
of the backpacks
into the shade at the river

there's a small hard body
scooped in sand
at my feet —
a pale oval stone
            I talk to egg:
            anyone could have found you
            accidental as a lover
            oval as my inner mouth

the Toyota tracks up a gully
on to the contour benched above the river

going in the direction of Mt Bulla Bulla
& Suggan Buggan River
            follow
a line, a track, a deviation
any alternative
in steep country
to find your egg

daughter stone

squat by an unlit fire
& the crystals of the stone
will encompass you

slide on a red river
low to the ground
as a creature is loved

like an arc or an exit
that returns you
to yourself

in a small turn
or a huge leap
now become human

the hand

bind my hand
and I shake it
in every direction
                   YOU LIE.
attached / tied
by twined spun-greasily
       hair
thinner & thinner the hair winds
as my hand spins

the stump of my hand in an old possum
pocket.
any defence
in this catchment:
Shades of Death — creek
northerly — Mt Trooper
& east up the river to another
— Slaughterhouse / creek
I could point in all directions

riddled with bullets
the ghost calls — TREATY?

avoidance place

I make a circle
to cross the river
at the beginning of Sandy Creek track

on the bare patch of ground
above the junction with the Snowy
I leave a small piece
of yellow quartz
next to the protector stone

I go around carefully
up Sandy Creek
& over
the ridge along from Mt Trooper
and down Joe Davis Creek

it takes four hours
to go around this one stone
which is a warrior stone
a fighting stone
& when I come back down-
stream to face it
the triple spears
        of stillness
        silence
        & distance
rush to grab me

I recross the river
re-enter the circle
& wait forever

crossing / ford II

at Burnt Hut crossing
I look for the long oval stone
in the fast river
the cleared country is above me
like clouds

I look for its reflection

I want to bring you down
                down to bones
                down to blood
                down to past country
down to stone

this stone is more than memory
it is strong
it resides in water

I look for its distinctive shape
in the river
I hear a list of names
                families
                massacres

the stone says:
        ignore the sorrow
        you ignore the healing

the stone has not been found

II

Biddi

search

once you had given me the directions
I could not look elsewhere
the further I went downriver —
I realised I'd come a long way
but according to the map
it was nowhere

I felt scared without the lineaments
of mapping: latitude & longitude
virtually unreal

I looked over the edge of all those
steep hills & cliffs
holding so much power
but what remains to be done with them?
how could they possibly be salvation?

I know the beauty in the small hollows
of ground when I turn
over the stones you have shown me
the rainbow colours lying in circles & swirls
as netting does over water
but if I am fish can I ever
be rainbow?

hillside vs river flow

you know from the design these places:
accurate & specific

the body charts topography
smoothly
as two small hills
I climb between
a circle & a point
over a pass to come
down onto the river
there's a single bent line
at the intersection
of Barrabilli Creek
& the west bend
turning towards
Milky Creek lookout
crosshatched above me
are small holes
in the red cliffs
& nearer
the perfectly straight line
of a waterfall
with a 1 metre drop
right across the river
sluices the diagram

I begin again:
8524 Jacobs River
FV 248087

8523 Murrindal
FV 271033
&
FV 249021

as I approach
the junction of the Snowy
& Suggan Buggan rivers
two low spurs disguise the exit
entrance/ the body recognises
the design
I continue walking
& the disguise is forgone
before I reach it

Biddi

we make love
before I leave
for Tongaroo junction

following an old track
along the riverbank
towards Willis Biddi

I feel the other things
that come to here:
no expectations
no sorrow

moving through the pines
in & out of sight
of a rock outcrop
on the opposite bank

cleft & circle
where the river turns
at the mouth of Willis Biddi

I splash in the shallows
going past the cleft
the hood widens
opening like renewal

the four men camped there
wake next morning
feeling transformed overnight
into female

horse koan

the roan stallion
hunts his mares
away from me
up the Willis Biddi

I follow the sandy
horse trail
out of the sun
towards Pinch Mountain

I pass axe blazes
on white-box trees
all the way
back down again

she-wolf

on her return
my sister brings a mask
the skin stretched tight
over its mouth & face
across a bone frame

she is starving
but unable to feed
her dugs dried
& unsuckled

since then she has herself
flesh
& a cavernous home

she has brought tidbits
for her nieces
scraps of fur
they nuzzle
and sniff at the distant
icy steppes

behind the skin of the mask
I become her imagination
milk bathes my eyes
& the children are drinking

bloodstones

a day's walk below the border
the stones begin
talking

            a
small reddy-pink stone
mush & pulpy
living as brain
would say
time to halt here

            a
slender oblong on the bend
below the helipad
pink-red & white speckles
suggests the blood
of my daughters
& when will I return to them

            a
larger speckled red-pink
palm stone — size
of a hand
carrying arrival
in late afternoon

now all the humans
have gone away/home
accompanied by their voices

I have forgotten them

the stones are like words
& I dare not take them up

the river draws me nearer
to a sound
underneath the water

Steeltrap

out along Turnback
Peacock & Gander
have gone
imitating the hunter's multiples
far-fetched & roaming

from this high up on the ridge
direction takes
automatically from the air
as speed does

the shale splits vertically
to the river
& vision goes
clear north
to the range behind S.B. junction

when I look down
I can see the striations
& darker hollows marked
on the sandy
river bed by waterflow

strong as illusion the dream works
its way into landscape:
having descended the spur
I look back up along Turnback
thinking this poem
was once about horses

nostalgia smoke

sniff is a dangerous quantity
but closer to home than you
ever shall be
arranging this damned godswill:
move the ladder closer
                (a dream goes up)
the toeholds slip
& the mountainface is an incorrect
vantage —
scarp & crevice
I reason: the fire
has yet to be identified

the gap

with no-death as the strata
& a rock-filled hole
we could be there
                    I implore you
don't forget your runners
& the trace remaining
on the sheet-wet sand
                    gather them up
you have nothing
to write on
but the lay of land
makes a nice fiction
so you can rest
your head
on the frontage just above
the thud of waves

figure eight

making two attempts to enter
the Snowy
meets the Brodribb
east of lakes Wat Wat & Corringle

it is a bright yellow morning
over the green slope
the two girls run

should I be forgiven
for not wanting them
to come closer/ their happiness

reflecting upon
the lake surface
like the thousand birds
I look down on
from the headland

their noise
raising me up
from the water

Long Point / lower Snowy

one metre in diameter
the sphere is a place
to stand in
smaller than the sun
gone
overhead to my left

the water goes around
on three sides/ Halt
I heard:
the flute of the goat boy
my sister brought
back from Europe
for the new year
further downstream
my mother's voice
over very hot sand
(the wine is the colour
of the willows)
in the shade there are bits
of my other relatives
talking

sentimental the goat
boy runs up
& down the other
side of the riverbank
bending wattles
a red hat over his genitals
we watch from the shade
taking turns

while someone minds
the children
to pad up the sandbank
to the sphere
falling inwards
to the lukewarm water

raft / Little River junction

the children fret
on the riverbank
under the shade
of an old tarp
& willow branches
I bend & weave
& knot
coloured wool
for the smallest
to pull on
the river
is too deep
to let them go
on their own
my sister
is passively helpful
we hold them
in the river for hours
I raft in & out
on anger
that night
it rains
& everything cools
next morning
I cross the river
to the conical mountain
& climb to the memorial
at nearly the top
to somebody's mate
from a walking club
his ashes still husking
his spirit around
the oldest kurrajong
I've ever seen
to the wasted rhythm
of doggerel

Boloco

inside a square of pine trees
halfway to Paupong
I find the other side
of my family: the lineage
lying north/south towards
the valley
& the stony upper ground
of the Snowy

how weighty their greeting is
I thought
among the plastic
flowers & white cockatoo feathers
they have landed me so

stance pattern III
cup

the growing moon goes down
behind the Turnback

the day's congested heat accumulates
in the steep V of the valley

the cumulo-nimbus engage their dense
function: forming & traversing

to strike & thunder
a thousand feet above the Snowy

I cross the river in the dark / bleed
a small trickle squatted on a log

the wind arrives, narrow as a tree
& soft

I cup up & empty out
like a stance for tomorrow

crossing / ford III
saddle

via the flare
of brumbies & the weedy

trench of an old sawmill
around the red gravelly

slopes west of the river
wheel tracks

circle in on themselves
slice & turn

in the sand
before the deep ford

at Biddi
black water & zen rocks

I wade through
where the pool empties:

narrowest & swiftest

dozer tracks cross the ridges
veering south-west

along a spur
towards Pigeon House

I go up to a saddle
where the light keeps

swallow

on top of Pigeon House
there is no fear
of flying
down, down, down
I want to go
the cliff edge
scrapes my fear
this is where
I let my sister
fall from me
the last wisps
of acrimony
spiralling up
to intersect
the flight path
of the Forestry plane
back & forth above me
over to Byadbo Mountain

I circle my camp
& the small fire
with stones
two young ones in colour
like sisters
or daughters
outside the circle
they are never to be in it
but they cover the opening
I draw them apart
for love

Farmers Creek

on the river bend
opposite Farmers Creek
an old man in black trousers, braces
& a clean white shirt
stands over a youth
kneeling in the sand

red dirt runs in little deltas
out over the sandbar
from the campsites behind the trees

I look down from my precarious rock
place
at the old man who in blessing
or baptism
touches the boy's head
lightly
then arranges the branch
of a single Snowy River wattle
close by
for transubstantiation
or the camera's eye

wood fish

at Balley Hooley
the canoeists strip
their thick black skins
down to underpants
I go around them
to the codfish pool
full of intent
as any old horseman
I move upstream
but the nettles deter me
the old cod watches
from the hillside
I throw
a small white stone
to introduce myself
the wind flecks
& cuts
the surface
of the big pool
not scouting
just dreaming
a wood fish rolls
over in the sand
near me

Byadbo

the weather glides out
of my bones
growing shorter & shorter
the sun folds me up
for winter
no thought
no memory

I throw the bones
for good luck
as they twist
see how chance falls
already rain
at the headwaters
surges downstream
perhaps a few more times
I may cross the river
to Byadbo

stone masks the ghost

so this big stone
brings the ghost
I've become too fragile
hearing this big ghost's
stone perspective

I move into the river
stop breathing
forced by the current
towards deeper water

cast out
I roll over
change species
and the story
hardens into stone

III

Gift

en/trance S.B. River

I carry two stones down river
from Willis
like my daughters
in each hand
to take a snake home

coiled
in my solar plexus
have I acted unwisely?

is this second best
to the ancient
search
for intimacy?

looking, looking — this stone or that?
no reply
yet they go with me
as if in accord, our willingness
matched

but in my heart
the hole is still there
like a shadowy love
moving through my vision:
I know you
but no-one is there

surely there could have been no harm
in asking:
where is the entry place?
but whom should I have asked?

you reassure me
that the colours of your rainbow-sleek skin
are always there
& in the whirlpool below camp
I can cast this song down

safe camp

by these pools of water
anyone could be like Christ
J. or the coloured snake

clean that worn-out soul

then start walking
anywhere downstream
to a smoky fire
exultant as the mountains

appear out of sunlit fog

land: your quote

female being / nothing place
oh mother — these knobbly rocks
        you gave me
I observe them
why should they be gifts?

after carrying each one
I'm more of you
than any birth
initiates
a form of belonging

land — having undertaken
the task
is it my undoing
that the vista should open
like surprise?

redness

you suck on my tongue
like a pink-red stone
I bring back for you

as I found it
marked faintly on it
are the eyes & mouth
of a red mask

as you rub against me
the eyes become tiny
& the mouth
a pale triangle

till the mask becomes
featureless
disappears into touch

the redness of the mask
grows
increasingly obvious

returning to the river
I leave the stone
& the image of the stone
is free to travel with me

stance pattern IV
718

I stand on the saddle of the mountain
in the midst of through traffic:
hawks & horses
& versions of the spirit

they go along & over
the end of the mountain top

I turn towards my sister
who has placed herself to the south
overlooking the river
step to one side
& lay my body down

in the shade I sleep
a sleep I've waited years for

I stand up
& step back
into the line along the mountain top

open my arms & extend them
into the stance
which brings forever

fanning & spreading out

this belly
     mother I am
where the landscape spreads
& fans out
not everywhere (am I)
               but here
I am motherness
myself
not other

beyond those low hills
east of the river
I do not go
as mother
but completely another
where the influence
of landscape
has altered
towards the back range
laying out tracks
as on the palm of a hand
& the aspect I approach
is perseverance

handmade
for ros

I

the gift of the beautiful woman
woos me like a rose-coloured mountain
or the transformation of a wound

give give give
sometimes she gives it away
sometimes she keeps it for herself

she renews it by inhabiting
the bend on the river
coming up against
herself & covered with grief

II

the power acts
& I swing
a burning stick in circles
in front of me
going through the opening
to call someone up river
five minutes before utter darkness

from Reedy

along Biddi bank
the soft earth
has been pounded
to powder
by horse mobs
foraging for green
tips along the river

after the long walk
from Reedy
in the last sweat
of the season
we backpack past
chewing on little bits
of coffee beans

gyre

I come off the dry hill
to the sound of water:
Gattamurh camp at the base of the ranges
smells damp & dank of men
& their sacks of grain hang from the rafters of
    the old hut

I leave the site quickly
following the valley down
past horse skulls & leg bones

crossing over
to a grassy flat
at the junction of Gattamurh & Shades of Death creeks
I splash a pebble in Shades of Death
there are droplets of water on my hands like blood
and the beastie appears: man warning
& a terrible smile

in this place she grows gigantic
feeding on horse heads & human thigh bones

under the cover of trees
I go through the sweet scented country
along Gattamurh Creek
an animal beats the earth
resonating

at the bottom of the valley
Gattamurh curves out to the Snowy
the gyre of the old lady
squats over me
she is the crazy one

who slips into your madness
when choices are stretched too far apart

I step out into the blue sky
& the raw state
as if weeping me

at night the old woman returns
wearing colours
& offers
to eat up my deaths

she looks like me

'she is big
she takes up half the world
        or more
she wears a triangular dress
like in a child's drawing
it is rainbow-hued
her arms extend straight out
from her body
and her hands & fingers are wide open
like stars
her hair & eyebrows are dark
there is no smile
she says a big YES
& NO
I can see her
breasts through the dress —
one for each child
she has fed me endlessly
she kept me alive
& I'm scared stiff of her'

stringbag

I retrieve
the dead body of a child
from the river

place it in my stringbag
to carry
across the river

as weighty
as stones
from the river bed

I bury her under warm
sand
on the river bank

carry home
my stringbag
with water in it

Rocky Conical Peak

a cone of she-oaks, kurrajong & xanthorrhoea
on a barish peak

Bald Hill trail to the river

I camp on a ledge
above the water
a little downstream from Slaughterhouse Creek
my children to the west of me

from a long way below
I stand watching
looking up
through long-leaved box
& cypress pine
at the one who waits:
the conical power
of all earth beneath

a sandbar juts into the river
below my tent
I push two slim sticks
of driftwood into the sand
in a line towards the fire:
love is the maker
as the hands which form clay

I turn away & she follows
nothing is ever buried:
beyond love & fear
I find the no-name of the universe

upstream / south

my family wait for me
on the Paupong
I cross the river again
to go up Milligans Mountain
just south
but upstream
from where we camp
I follow a brumby track
up along a spur
all the way
to the highest peak
it is still cold
in the morning light
past a nest of horses
I come over the mountain
opposite Rocky Conical Peak

moving down
I come out
onto a grassy point directly above
Reedy Creek junction
into a quality like shimmering
or unbelief
the beauty glimmering
at a very subtle level:
the entrancing faculty of landscape

at the mouth of Reedy Creek
two rock pinnacles
& a low plateau of sand
face into the river

I wait among the grasses
unbidden / hidden
above the wall of ghosts
then go down into the valley

at the river
though the valley is deep
it is open
the feeling of elevation
hovers over me
with my back to the rocks
I squat on the sand
an image appears
enters like an imprint
a pattern that lasts
I can hold it & see it
as an oval platter
carried in front of me
or place it within
& cherish

like something given back
after a long time away
I carry it with me to the Paupong

wish

breathe
into the atoms of nature
& nothing changes
except the wish
& its fulfilment

song: to the heart

may the spirit come to me
may my heart be empty
of the past
may the song be true
may the song carry me there

having appeared
along a ridge
above Barrabilli Creek

the spirit comes down
like horses
to drink at the river

over low saddles
between the hills
a little east of north
through the cypress pines
swishing

to the green creek bank
above the Snowy
travelling continuously
it is already there

the way animals travel
particular routes
persuaded by
the slant of hills
the pleasure of water
the lower land
approaching the river

along paths
formed in the memory
of landscape:
instructive & direct
as a mandala

for the practice
like prayer or art
in the perception of
the spirit
& the places
it is travelling

Notes

karst. The two quotations, given by P. D. Gardiner in his *Gippsland Massacres* (Warrigal Education Centre, 1983, pp. 74 and 31), are from articles in two separate issues of *The Gap*: respectively, from 'The Macleod family and the founding of Bairnsdale' by John D. Adams (1967, p. 7) and 'Butcher's Ridge — The Slaughterhouse' by Miss A. McRae (1966, p. 55).

Steeltrap. In 1843 two stallions, Peacock and Gander of the Steeltrap breed, were brought by Davey O'Rourke to Black Mountain and later run on an area now known as Turnback. See H. Stephenson, *Cattlemen & Huts of the High Plains* (Viking O'Neil, 1988, p. 47).

travelling
alone together

in the footsteps of Edward John Eyre

Miriel Lenore

Miriel Lenore was born in Boort, Victoria, and educated in Bendigo and Melbourne. She worked as a plant breeder, student counsellor, teacher, and as a writer and editor of Fijian church publications. After twenty-two years in Fiji, she made Adelaide her base and began writing poetry during a Women's Studies course in 1984.

Her first collection, *The Lilac Mountain*, appeared with two others in *Across the Gulf* (Friendly Street Poets, 1992); *sun wind & diesel* was published by Wakefield Press in 1997, the title poem having won the Red Earth Award in 1994. With Mary Moore, she has written the text of *Masterkey*, Moore's multimedia adaptation, for the 1998 Perth and Adelaide Festivals, of a novel by the Japanese writer Masako Togawa.

for Julia, Claire, Rachel and Robin

Acknowledgements

Some of these poems have been published in *ars poetica*, *Hobo*, *Meanjin* and *Muse*, and broadcast over 5UV.

Too many people have helped in this project to be acknowledged by name. They include librarians, local historians, those involved in the re-enactment, friends and family and my long-suffering writing group. I owe a special debt to the women and crew of my Eyre tour who will not find themselves in this book, though I have borrowed various events and conversations with gratitude.

Thanks are due to Arts South Australia for a grant which assisted in the writing of this book.

*on the whole [Wylie] had behaved extremely well
under all our troubles since we had been travelling
together alone.*

Edward John Eyre: *Journals*, 17 May 1841

travelling alone together

Contents

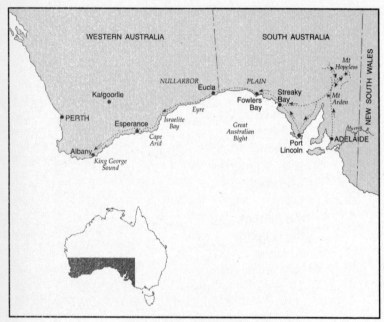

Eyre's journey, 1840–41

Introduction

When I joined a 'John Eyre Expedition' in 1993, a tour following Eyre's journey from Adelaide to Albany, I had no interest in, and little knowledge of, the young explorer. I wanted to visit stone arrangements on the Nullarbor and this seemed the easiest way. My first surprise was to discover that all eight tourists were senior women. As we wandered and camped across the plain and along the coast, I began to compare our journey with the little I knew of Eyre's, and this project began.

A grant from the South Australian Department for the Arts and Cultural Heritage enabled me to retrace Eyre's route again. On this trip, I learnt of the re-enactment walk organized in 1991 by the Royal Western Australian Historical Society to celebrate the sesquicentenary of Eyre's best-known Australian feat, the 1500-kilometre trek from Fowlers Bay to Albany. Three people repeated the whole walk but many joined it for different stages. Seven plaques were erected along the route, and nearby townships became closely involved. Travelling again through these townships, it became clear to me that whatever his other roles in history, Eyre continues to be a growing part of our mythology.

He has long held an honoured position in Australian history. In southern Australia, we see his name on lakes, mountains, roads, streets, parks, a peninsula. For us at primary school he was an example of courage, daring and endurance, and his Nullarbor journey, which he saw as honourable failure, takes its place among our other valorizations of failure.

Edward John Eyre, the son of an English clergyman with an ancient family history, came to Australia in 1834, aged seventeen. After a short career as a grazier in the Hunter region and the Monarto, he overlanded cattle and sheep to Melbourne and Adelaide and also from Albany to York.

In 1839, from his base in Adelaide, he explored the Flinders Ranges and the peninsula that would bear his name. Having persuaded the South Australian settlers that their projected search for a stock route to the West was impossible, in 1840 he was given charge of an expedition to explore the country towards the centre of Australia, still unknown to the British. Stopped by salt lakes, he went west, reducing his party from eight to five at Fowlers Bay, before setting off for Albany in defiance of instructions. After great privations and difficulties, his overseer Baxter was killed by two of the party, who fled. The remaining two, Eyre and his Nyoongar companion Wylie, after continuing struggles and a providential respite on a whaling ship, eventually walked into Albany in July 1841.

From September 1841 until his departure from Australia in 1845, Eyre was a highly regarded Resident Magistrate and Protector of Aborigines at Moorundie on the River Murray, earning a reputation for preserving the peacefulness of the district and for his concern for the wellbeing of the Aboriginal people.

For twenty years Eyre served in senior administrative posts in New Zealand and the West Indies. In 1865, as Governor-in-Chief of Jamaica, he imposed martial law when rioting erupted. He was recalled to England after excesses of cruelty by the British, and charged. He was acquitted three times of related charges but lived in seclusion for the remaining decades of his life. He wrote of himself as 'a public servant who conscientiously believed and still believes that he only did his duty under circumstances of great emergency and very grave responsibility — and the discharge of which has entailed upon him professional ruin'. His last letter to his daughter regrets his inability to provide for her — 'it has not been in my power to do so'. Between the *If I Can* of his honoured family motto and those last words lies a troubled life, shaped by his times, his genes, his own story. Although this project deals only with his 1840–41 expedition, his later life colours, for me, everything he does.

north

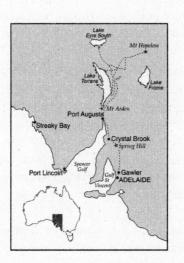

departure

someone smashes into my car
as we wait

a bad omen
though on Eyre's first expedition from Adelaide

a drunken Baxter fell off his horse into an open cellar
yet *all went well*: good land was found

our departure point
a grey deserted building losing the letters of its name

but close to the same Government House
whose earliest functions included in 1840

Eyre's third departure: *dejeuner a la fourchette*
with Governor Gawler and important citizens

who rode with *Mr Scott, myself, and two native boys*
carrying the Union Jack *the ensign of our country*

made by the ladies & presented by Captain Sturt:
you have to carry it to the centre of a mighty continent,

there to leave it as a sign to the savage
that the footstep of civilized man has penetrated so far

the crowd's cheers made the horses bolt
over the bridge & up the North Adelaide hill

we get no such boisterous send-off   the Troop Carrier
with its closed trailer forty-five minutes late

eight *retired* women   two crew with one to come
following the steps of a 25-year-old explorer

seeking landscapes not land

decisions

Meg thinks the reserve driver
should have the best seat each day

& Elsie agrees with her
Elsie always agrees with her

Claire disagrees
we are the ones who paid

we reach a compromise:
Tom will not sit in front

but stay in the first seat of the back
as we move around the bus each day

no-one is fully satisfied   that's democracy

Eyre had no more love for democracy
than army commanders

who must lead
though others take the consequences

ruthless with any challenge
he fought his servants in court

once only   on the cliffs
he granted Baxter's plea to stop

an unfortunate decision for Baxter

Devil's Glen

The country below was broken with a hundred little hills and glens of steep ascent and thro' the whole was winding a strongly running stream connecting deep large ponds. The whole seemed so wild and fantastic that I named it the Devil's Glen . . .

Hell's Gate now to the locals   how do so many
plots of earth become satanic possessions?

some mysterious quality or merely a hedging of bets?
(the last river had honoured a bishop)

but why does the devil get the best landscapes
as he is said to have the best tunes?

on the valley floor
a chimney remains of a shepherd's hut:

a place for Old Nick to retire

Mircowie (clear water)

two hours out
for us a welcome stop
for Eyre the *pretty stream* he named:

The water was excellent, so pure and clear,
and the whole so forcibly reminded me
of the beautiful bubbling brooks at home
that I at once named it the Crystal Brook

today heroic red gums stand their ground
along an empty creek bed

in the Old Bakehouse museum
a pioneer's heavy cart recalls the gear
explorers dragged through scrub
before plastic & aluminium

smooth river stones regimented
into a monument by the ford
announce that young Eyre
passed this way   headed north

his cumbersome luggage including
a boat for the inland sea

accomplishment

on Spring Hill slopes he'd found a dying man
left without food or fire to perish

almost unconscious of our presence the man
stared upon us with a vacant unmeaning gaze

Eyre knew there was no other choice
(the man cannot be carried   the tribe must leave)

but for the young man   such a tragedy
he records it twice for different years

careless it seems of his own death
why was this so memorable?

for an old man whose time had come
letting go might be his powerful work

like Buddhist monks who turn
their faces to the wall & cease to breathe

or the Ngaanyatjarra woman who begged
to be taken to her place & left awhile

when her kin returned
she had accomplished death

death is the last enemy for St Paul — & me
but other insights wait:

Teilhard's *diminishment* perhaps to learn
or Dickinson's *Another way — to see —*

Port Augusta

the prospect being generally cheerless and barren in the extreme, nor did the account given by Mr Brown of his ascent [in 1802] tempt me . . . to view the uninteresting prospect he had seen from the summit of that hill . . .

approaching the town
a bus with LOST as its destination

a sign saying PORT AUGUSTA MICE
and a roadside stop with free coffee

we're ready for lunch
first chance to introduce ourselves

a task Jim hasn't done but we're shy & quiet
sit at separate tables with sandwiches & tea

Ilse begins to shop   buys a new hat books postcards
a carved goanna & a tiny dot painting

a pattern she will repeat in each shopping place
already has double the luggage allowed

she hums to herself   smiling
                        has saved for this all year

Wadlata

we see the windmill first
poking through the roof of the new tourist centre —
Gateway to the Outback

we climb the front steps
past two corrugated-iron tanks
almost blasphemy to find they are toilets

only half an hour Jim says
we hurry to explore the display
past geology botany & the first inhabitants

we reach a plaster model of Eyre with mud slurry
for the dusty look   gaunt   bent   an old man
(who left Australia before thirty)

a heavy telescope beside him
the heroic explorer shields his eyes
from the light he shares with Stuart & Giles
& Sturt (hauling *his* boat towards that inland sea)

on the wall Lawson & Paterson sanctify the bush
now starred with mines of coal & uranium

Claude

the last member of the party
arrives with the smallest bag

travelling light
is an ancestral skill

he makes for the back of the van
& stays there

refusing to join in
our daily rotation of seats

my old discomfort surfaces:
he must not be excluded

then I recall a Fiji scene:
rather than sit at the table for whites

I insist on joining
the women on the floor

we speak in a halting mix
of English & Fijian

as I leave I hear the room
erupt in energetic talk

sticks & stones

Eyre had no such troubles
Claude would be *the native*

or one of *our sable friends*
occasionally a *sable fellow traveller*

twenty years ago following the USA
we might have used *black*

now an Aboriginal woman from the east
has offered *koori* as the global word

Claude is outraged   he doesn't say
imperial takeover but the words hang

he says *we're nungas*
in the west they're nyoongars or wongais

up north it's anangu or even blackfella
surely we can name ourselves

I have to agree:
a Scot doesn't want to be called English

but must I use the awkward *indigenous Australian*
or can I say *blackfella* without blushing?

the red handkerchief

terrible the silence of the journals

the explorers' anguish sometimes finds words
the cries of the terrified are muffled

searching for water near Mt Deception
Eyre   first white man there & his *native boy*

met with a party of native women and children,
but could gain no information from them.

They would not permit me to come near them,
and at last fairly ran away,

leaving at their fire
two young children who could not escape.

he finds two kangaroo skins full of water
as he examines their camp

having taken *some of the water, I tied a red handkerchief*
round one of the children, as payment for it

next day passing the camp he *called to see*
if the children had been taken away

no   still there   in a hole the elder had scraped
in the ashes of the dead fire

They were alarmed when they saw me,
and would take nothing I offered them.

The child around whom I had tied the handkerchief,
had managed to get it off and throw it to one side.

Eyre knows he cannot care for them:
decides the parents *must* return

Under this impression, I put the handkerchief
again round the oldest child, and tying it firmly, I left them.

coming back a fortnight later Baxter checks the camp
to find the children gone   the place abandoned

the red handkerchief of *such fearful enchanters*
left at the camp

and the whole plain around
had been strewn with green boughs

well-treated

*I had among other matters requested him, if he found any natives
in the neighbourhood, to try to get one up to the camp and induce
him to remain until my return, that we might, if possible, gain some
information as to the nature of the country or the direction of the
waters.*

so Baxter chased a group of men & women
*came up with one of the females
took her a prisoner to the camp*

he *could gain no information from her*
though she pointed to east & north-west
when asked by signs about water

*After keeping her for two days, during which,
with the exception of being a prisoner,
she had been kindly treated,
she was let go
with the present of a shirt and a handkerchief.*

*It was to revenge this aggression
that the natives had now assembled;
for which I could not blame them.*

who has studied the place of
the handkerchief in British exploration?

the Irish overseer

a sailor's son from County Down
farm bailiff good carpenter & cooper
before his transportation

seven years with Eyre on Woodlands farm
& overlanding stock
a trusted aide in every expedition

Eyre praised *his courage, prudence, and fidelity*
excused his drinking (immaterial out bush)
yet in the journal seldom used his name

he is *the overseer*
only gentlemen have names
the rest are men or natives

my great-grandmother
was a parlourmaid from Tandragee
near County Down

for Baxter
serving the righteous English
I have a family feeling

until I remember that captured woman

celebration

against the blue
       backdrop of the Flinders
a railway links
the Leigh Creek coalfields
to the furnaces of Port Augusta

easy to miss the sculpture on the plain
under Mt Arden:
a train wheel fixed on a tilted rail
to honour Eyre
         who led the way

this most unlikely of his monuments
was a Bicentennial project
      of the local primary school
where the Aboriginal pupils
could not compete in races
unless they wore shoes
        they did not own

under Mt Arden (i)

the wild sad cry of swans
brings Eyre from his tent
their northward flight
promising that inland sea
whose glitter would be salt

under Mt Arden (ii)

on my sixty-seventh birthday
I walk in the open with Helen & Claire

nothing to slow us but daypacks
we head for walls of rock
so misty-blue far off
severely white & red up close

uncertain of Mt Arden   we photograph
all likely peaks   stand where we think
young Eyre set up his base
before the failed northern trek

(under these hills   at this reliable water
his goal was still attainable)

horses gallop at us hoping for feed
their pace & flared nostrils
a warning of danger
we stop & outface them   hiding our fear
until they move away

as we talk of *our* lengthening trek
we long for such easy success
with other dangers
my goal is to walk through red gums
towards the astonishing hills

learning to know when it's time to turn in

peninsula

fenced land

for the Bicentennial five men on horseback
re-enact Eyre's ride through Nawu country

when he penetrated the land
they now possess and farm

my school history book showed a series of maps
beginning with Australia all black

then a white arc extended from Sydney
a bigger arc after 1813

more white with Sturt Oxley Mitchell & the amazing
Human Hovell before Eyre Leichhardt & Stuart

surprising how each slender route
so much enlarged the white

surprising how much black dissolved
with each explorer's trail

the map has long been uniform
when the horsemen repeat Eyre's Peninsula rides

his precise route now impossible to follow:
fenced land has lost its music   as the Adnyamatana say

Iron Knob

We had a very bad stony road today, consisting principally of quartz and ironstone . . . It was through this dreary region I had left my overseer to take his division of the party when we separated . . .

a scatter of roofs under a chewed-up red hill
just south of the range
Eyre named for the industrious Baxter

hard to keep the iron out of your soul
when it's at your back all day
a relentless sun to set it on fire

though ancient rough Mt Brown
is an ethereal peak
across the remaining trickle of the Gulf

the women are tired
as they push babies up hot streets
past empty shops and fibro cottages

tired as I've seen
Nimbin women tired
but here no rainbows fill their eyes

Mt Sturt

stand on the granite slopes of Minipa
& catch your breath at blue peaks
                floating on the plain below

a hazy blue   not Virgin's robes
love-in-the-mist perhaps
                the *Blue Sturts* to the locals

Eyre honoured the Governor first —
the range is Gawler's
                (was it a prudent move?) —

& then his mentor & explorer friend:
did these blue peaks remind him
                of that melancholic man?

the *chipped idol*
never saw his lovely mountain

in retreat to England
the friends strolled
                over separate green fields

did they miss that *frisson* of danger?
as fighter pilots keep for ever (so I'm told)
                a certain restlessness

Cannon Gorge

columellar basalt
protrudes into the valley
could be
candy sticks
a pincushion
angry echidnas
but the man who named it
saw guns

Sturt's desert pea

named first for Dampier after 1699
Clianthus formosus was a happier choice:
> beautiful glory flower

though others long before had called it
> *malu kurakura*
the eye of the kangaroo

just past Mt Allalone in the Gawlers
Eyre first recorded it in South Australia:

a most splendid creeping plant
the flower bright scarlet
> *with a rich purple centre*

floral emblem for the driest State
it flaunts dark lips beside desert tracks

there is a legend too of faithful lovers
& spilt blood
> more Camelot than Kokatha

now it features in supermarket specials
can be grown
> from seed soaked at tepid heat

recently two Adelaide banks
battled in court to own the symbol of
> such dangerous sexuality

history

he had been here last year   his tracks
still visible between the waterholes he knew
                    & landmarks he had named:

mountains interspersed with lakes
as if a giant hand scooped out earth
                              then dropped it

Lake Hamilton honours George his friend
Mounts Hope & Misery —
                    we get the point

but *a high bare-looking detached range
named by me from its shape,*
                    Mount Wedge

becomes in a different book a peak
John Darke named five years later
                    for his uncle Harry Wedge

Lake Calpatanna

we pitch in drizzling rain
our Agincourt of tents
on the moonscape
border of the lake:
salt   samphire   limestone
& a singing fence

the sky clears
as we sit around the fire
talking of stars & stalagmites
while the men cook

campaign-weary
we fall into our beds
except for Lorna   who
in a raincoat for the cold
sits outside her tent
observing Jupiter's moons
counting satellites
watching for the Orionids

Murphy's Haystacks

on the hill named Oakfront
scrappy trees bend under the wind from the sea

& squat stone guardians
surround a helmet Henry Moore might shape

fifteen hundred million years of wind & rain
have carved this Hiltaba granite

into a sound-shell where a distant car is heard
louder than Rachmaninov

Claire asks if Murphy once lived here
or is the name an ethnic joke?

identity

*I rode forward in advance to the depot near Streaky Bay, where I
... was delighted to find the party all well, and everything going on
prosperously... Around the camp were immense piles of oyster shells,
[and my men's] strong and healthy appearance shewed how well such
fare had agreed with them.*

i

this town of seaweed & mallee has named
its parish church for St Augustine of Hippo

ii

as waterholes to Eyre   public toilets to tourists
our progress regulated by our bladders
we stop for lunch on a windswept beach beyond
that point the Dutchman reached in 1627

iii

the streaks in the water intrigued Flinders
but were they shoals seaweed or the play of light?

forty years later Baxter & the men
eat cartloads of oysters from the Bay

waiting weeks *in dire anxiety* for Eyre to come
with supplies for their westward expedition

we drive to their Cooeyana well
surprised to find in a sheet of limestone

wooden posts around a hole *just large enough for a pint pot*
yet supplying eight men thirteen horses forty sheep

the roadside entrance is flanked by a metal plaque
shared by Eyre & the Bratten plough once used for roads

iv

Eyre hurried from Cooeyana twice
in duty and in honour bound
unlike the curator of the town's museum
who left only for war   returned on divine mission:

as army doctors hovered over him he had
a vision of gates & Jesus coming out to say
Alec go back there's work to do
so Alec came back & did it:

years of resolute collecting —
gigs & ploughs restored & burnished
scarifiers   the poison cart
the horsedrawn stick-picker

Mudge's Royal Mail coach with its rough sapling shaft
repaired on the track by Tom Mudge himself
Mrs Sylvia Birdseye's Straight Eight Nash
first road service to the Bay
and the reconstructed Kelsh cottage
which won a national prize

as Alec kneels to replace a tiny missing part
Claire remembers a German etching: *work is prayer*

generosity

the roughest travel so far met
this worse than desert region

made lighter by Wilguldy
an *intelligent cheerful old man*
who first time on a horse leads them
the shortest way to water

lucky that extra day of rest at Smoky Bay
after the axes hacked a path from Cooeyana
enabling them to meet the friendly Wirangu
who guided them to Fowlers Bay

And Eyre is grateful: *the best conducted,
most obliging natives I ever met with*

who offered the water to their guests
& wouldn't drink from it themselves
without first asking permission

*Surely this genuine hospitality
may well put to the blush
his more civilized brethren*

who *occupy his country,
and dispossess him of his all*

who knows?

when I tell my friends
he let the young boys sleep in his tent
they roll their eyes and nod their heads —
to be expected now I guess

no no I say it's not like that
such an honourable chap young Eyre
so concerned for his family name
I think they were just pampered pets to him

one does wonder about sex
on these long expeditions
Eyre the Victorian gentleman says nothing
except for his judgement on whalers

yet he did unusual things:
bribing their parents to leave the boys with him
taking the youngest for no clear reason
on that last desperate walk

I heard (though can't believe)
that a Maralinga man insists
his grandfather slept with Daisy Bates
after that   who knows?

enough of admirals

lucky that Flinders stayed along the coast
we have enough of admirals & friends

French names had style but a shorter life
Lacepede & Champagny
                        now Kingston & Port Lincoln

the inland names of the Banggarla
continue to sing:
            Yardea Minipa Warramboo
            Yaninee Coodlie Wudinna
            Waddikee Caralue Pinbong

on the dry windswept hills after Penong
we pass a bare farm named Somerset

wisdom

guided around the head of the Bay
Eyre arrives first at the waterhole
surprises women & children
roasting snakes & lizards on the fire

They were much afraid and ran away

he realizes how few women they have seen
surmises this has been deliberate
perhaps sealers & whalers have been here?
a reason too the men are willing guides?

Old Wilguldy, however, appeared
to be less scrupulous on this point,
and frequently made
very significant offers on the subject

we assume young Eyre is not
to be tempted
or is that what he hopes
we assume?
                    in any case
the women were wise to run away

fool's mate

halfway round Fowlers Bay
Eyre camps under *many scrubby hills*
all of which commanded our position

uneasy at having *many well armed natives*
above him (in spite of their kindness)
he moves camp *to the hill next above them*

they also broke up camp
and took possession
of the next hill beyond us

now Eyre's move:
to *the highest hill we could find*

final move:
during the day the natives all left

a costly game —
never again would local people guide him

as he searched in misery for water
compelled to drink his horse's blood

depot 1841

i decision

one hundred days the men are camped
while Eyre attempts a northern course

impossible   he finally admits
will try now for a western route
he already knows is profitless —
anywhere but back

ii madness

is the Adelaide view of Eyre's plan
to travel west at the wrong time of year

he ignores the Governor's order to return
in the *Hero* & abandon *this mad attempt*

Eyre the youth who braved a flooded river
when he could barely swim

so many times
risked death by thirst & misadventure

lacks the courage to return to Adelaide
in what he sees as failure

iii the team

did any explorer's party boast
a higher proportion of Aborigines?
three out of five for the final push to Albany

Scott the gentleman is sent home
the overseer Baxter is asked to come
the natives have no choice:

Wylie the *intelligent young man* from Albany
may hopefully interpret
Neramberein can help with sheep & horses

and Cootachah ah Cootachah now twelve
has been four years with Eyre since small & naked
he left Mr Yalbone's party at the Goulburn

on this dangerous coast
where every pound carried is an extra risk
Three natives were more than I required

but Cootachah *had been with me several years;*
besides, he was so young and so light in weight
his presence could cause but little extra difficulty

25 February 1991

a barbecue & dance
farewell the walkers
a hundred & fifty years to the day
since Eyre's small band set off

Ceduna children have walked here
following Eyre & Wilguldy's path

a ship in the harbour becomes the *Hero*
to bring the Governor's letter   a mailbag   a flag
Mr Goss's special crock of wine
& a tin of soil from Eyre's Port Lincoln block
(still in his name on the council books)
to pour on land he once owned at Albany

three walkers set out for Albany
& thirty for the border
they cross a salt marsh & a plain
to the old homestead well   Eyre's second depot
so the leader from Ceduna thinks

his wife's mother was born near here
if the map is right

Fowlers Bay 1993

no barbecues or dances
only three or four houses in use
& a few closed-up weekenders

we park outside a pile of rubble
with a For Sale sign & a phone number

$12 000 we're told will buy it
though the dunes will soon march over

which may make it as famous
as Eucla's Telegraph Station under the sand
for its history is even more complex

we learn it was a pub   butcher shop   fish factory
since the town was laid out
& briefly given the name Port Eyre

a woman gathering quandongs
tells how a boy hanged himself in the ruins

playing cowboys & Indians
he slipped & the rope —
her hand slices across her throat

insufficient evidence

sand is blowing from the ridges
like snow from Manaslu
Claire scrambles up the high white dunes alone
hunting for the expedition's wells

tangled black polythene pipes
snake up & over the dunes
to the distant windmills in a hollow soak

now she sees how Eyre knew where to dig
snaps the depression with its tell-tale plants
& the windmills owned by each separate house
inspects a covered box-sized dam
so happy

a man in a cap saunters down the opposite slope
walks behind bushes   does not reappear
what is he doing   just here   just now
is he checking the windmill?
but he's not headed there
is he the odd-looking youth she met on the jetty?
is he just curious   or concerned?

she decides not to explore the further soak
nor follow the twisting pipes
makes straight for the road as the man follows

they walk separately down to the Bay
one case closed: insufficient evidence
one case closed: Eyre's well probably found

nullarbor

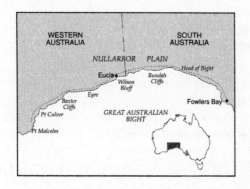

the dog fence

Eyre struggling for water & feed
had no trouble with fences

9600 kilometres of wire
to keep dingoes from the sheep

an obstacle for thirty-three walkers

rather than plod
to the distant gate & back

they clamber leap or straddle
the six-foot fence

from a support truck on one side
to a second on the other

a ballet performance the leader says

the dray

desperate yet again   Eyre
returns from another quest for water
to find the dray & its driver
surrounded by natives

the horses too weak
to move the dray further
their last water back twenty-two miles
they must bury their gear & quickly return

impossible while the Mirning watch   so they sit
Eyre *vexed and irritated beyond measure*
the natives coolly and calmly
with careless indifference lounging about

they move off once but return
before the caching can begin
eight hours are lost before they leave —
& the lives of Eyre's three best horses

he had thought of using force
(for we were all armed)
but cannot shoot those who
have been friendly
and who knew not the embarrassment
and danger which their presence caused us

misunderstanding

i

twenty-one miles from Head of the Bight
horses & men in drastic need of water

Eyre asks *our sable friends*
who point to sand drifts near the sea

& next day take the party there
over a dreadful heavy road

both groups are disappointed:

Eyre learns there is no water
the Mirning see no ship

ii

after a scorching day
the support truck arrives at sunset

bringing beer for the walkers
a drum of water for washing

having trudged over limestone & sand
the thirsty walkers prefer water

next day are violently ill
from weedkiller dregs in the drum

water still precarious gold

death

Distressing and fatal as the continuance of these cliffs might prove to us, there was a grandeur and sublimity in their appearance that was most imposing, and which struck me with admiration . . . It was indeed a rich and gorgeous view for a painter . . .

there has to be a death
the man from Sydney claims
it *is* a re-enactment

travelling with bottles of pills
he'd signed himself out of Callan Park
though no-one knew

on top of the great Bundah cliffs
he shouts
this is the place for my jump

the agitated leader declares
he is upsetting the women
radioes the police

& the man is taken away
no-one reminding him
Baxter was shot

Eyre's Well

beach at last
those white dunes promise water

did Eyre & the boys swim as they had before
on their terrible reconnaissance?
too early to frolic with whales

those long cigars that cruise with their babies
rolling & flipping & blowing
mocking the frenetic scramble of our age

when we arrive no whales are visible
that's nature says Claire
you can't make whales appear

Ilse says calves drink
two hundred litres of milk a day
we mothers sympathize

a brown depression behind a coastal dune
is marked on our map *Eyre's Well*
we picture his relief as he dug

or was it Baxter who shovelled?

later a Eucla man says
Eyre's well is further back —
we'll have to come again

phones

at every petrol stop
it's the toilets first
then the store for cool drinks
icecream & postcards

three hurry to the phones
ring *home*
for Meg a Melbourne suburb
for Lin a seaside town

for Lorna a friend over the desert
the thousand k seem close
only dunes & a plain between
same wavelength always

well   nearly always

Jeedara

we follow the old highway
past rockhole & cave

the Nullarbor serpent Jeedara
sings quietly from the blowholes

its cooling breath today masks
the fearsome power the Mirning felt

as roaring & sucking it snaked underground
from sea to plain and back

we enter a cave where handprints on the walls
speak of those earlier visitors who belonged

under a hole in the roof
the pile of rocks *could* have been put there

a mummified kangaroo is anchored upright
with a beercan in its paw

Elsie laughs in embarrassment
still takes a photograph

the great escape

the grader mounted as memorial
to the sealing of Eyre Highway in 1976
pays tribute to that epic journey
become the stuff of national myth:

EYRE & HIS FAITHFUL COMPANION,
   THE ABORIGINE WYLIE
SURVIVED HUNGER THIRST DESERTION
   AND DEATH
TO REACH ALBANY ON 7 JULY 1841

as proof of immortality
amongst the grader's casual graffiti
(AF   DF   Sam & Tina in a heart)
a scratched & rusting signature: *Ted Eyre 1841*

the engraving

Claude is an urban man
returning now to tribal country
hoping the land will speak to him

last year he found some tiny caves
full of strange power & danger
we must stay clear

next day he offers to show Lorna
engravings in those caves
she's thrilled   rock art a special interest

they scramble up the slope
to enter a cool shelter
under the escarpment crest

the wall is eroded with cracks & holes
Claude points to marks
she knows are only weathering

Mmm she mumbles   *could be*
then turns seawards to be forgiven
her complex dishonesty

or is it that he senses
some link to history
she cannot read?

next day Claude traces a human figure
in the escarpment stones
I think I see it Lorna says   learning nothing

the cave

her legs in turn cement & jelly
Lin can't step onto the iron ladder
down to the cave
though people are waiting

her quivering legs manage the first step
her palms & temples sweat
with tightened jaw
she crawls from rung to rung

the deep silence of the underground lake
is her reward

the only sound the plip of oars
as Jim rows her to a cavern
where candles glow from niches in the wall
it's a cathedral she whispers

then considers her words —
cathedrals at their best are like this cave

the climb to come
again will terrify — & be forgotten
the candles will stay with her

watched

The traces of natives were numerous and recent,
but yet we saw none.

all the way
through scrub &
along the Nullarbor
dark eyes
unseen
watched Eyre
so the story is told

it is easy
to believe:
he had failed
the Mirning twice
perhaps much more

not trusted as guides
now they would
only observe
& marvel at
incompetence

Border Village

when the Deputy Premier
flew in to unveil

the neat metal plaque
on its solid limestone block

the plaque   not properly attached
flipped over

was tied back on with string
so the media could finish filming

disappeared later that day
& hasn't been seen since

ask the publican someone suggests
(the pub is all there is at Border Village)

Barry is new
didn't know there was a plaque

a man glued to his corner
leaves his drink on the bar

comes back with the metal plate
we'll put it up says Barry

maybe —
the boulder has now disappeared

Wilson Bluff

how could Eyre scrambling terrified
around cliffs
at the 129th degree of longitude
know it would be a State boundary

so that in the one room telegraphists
received messages
& poked them through a hatch
for other operators to send on

or that councils and laws
would separate Pitjanjatjara relatives
by that imaginary line
drawn on their ground

or know that rabbits & the cats
brought in for their control
would free the stable dunes
to swallow a town

and that one of the re-enactment walkers
bending to pick up
an old telegraph insulator
would find it attached to its still-upright pole?

Eucla

what is this place? Delisser asked
pointing to the escarpment

Yer-cul-er the people replied
looking at Venus glowing huge over the cliffs

thus it became Eucla   though it is Jinyila
to those who say *Mirning* for *man*

standing on the great dunes that engulfed the town
Claire observes there is no scarp to the west

only as morning star would Venus hang above cliffs

the story begins to unravel
as she imagines a pre-dawn intimacy never spoken

Mundrabilla

this ant-eaten twelve-bore shotgun
badly damaged   flintlock missing

was found near the woolshed
& thought to be Eyre's (*it's the right age*)

brought back perhaps by the frightened boys
who killed the overseer

sent to the Adelaide museum
where the staff weren't very impressed

it could have a more sombre provenance
& belonged to McGill   founder of Mondra Bellae

a violently abusive man who shot the Mirning
gave them poisoned pudding

sand

Eyre discovered
the sage's advice
to walk lightly on the earth
is difficult in sand

Meg

in the smallest pause after meals
she leaves to wash the dishes

when we drive her away (*it's not your turn*)
she stands teatowel ready

Elsie is never far behind
they do everything together

skilful campers
they quickly choose the best tent site

fill their thermos before bed
for the 5 am cuppa (*to get us going*)

ready first   they make the men's lunches
as well as help them pack

Meg's quiet at the meal table & evening fire
so it surprises more

when she talks of longhouses in Kalimantan
& white-water rafting in Alaska

Meg doesn't go down the ladder at Weebubbie
we assume she wants to rest

next day at Abracowie cave
she jolts us with a white-tipped stick

(*my sight's quite bad
can't drive these days or see the birds*)

edges down the steep shale slope
beyond the entrance

apologizes for being slow
(*I'm like a snail with this new hip*)

that night Meg coaxes a fire
with wet wood & much blowing

stands drying our pants & shirts
her own already folded in her bag

wisps of grey escaping her woollen cap
are lit up by the firelight

Madura

stony & hot the tableland
we retreat to the petrol station's
cool drinks
postcards of swaggies parrots
                    & bush poems

Lorna sees *My Country*
                    by Dorothea Mackellar
this she must send to a friend
who had lampooned it
at the launch
of a post-modern text
                    to great applause

the young attendant
leaves oilcans & tins of grease
to sort through her purchases
                    reaches *My Country*

he smiles & his eyes sparkle
that's a wonderful poem he says
I recite it sometimes while I'm
                    cleaning up

Eyre Bird Observatory

*Our last drop of water was consumed this evening . . . [To] our great
relief fresh water was obtained at a depth of six feet from the surface,
on the seventh day of our distress . . .*

once called Eyre's Sandpatch
this break in the cliffs meant water
& then a telegraph station
now you can holiday here

on the littoral
near a tiny well in the limestone capping
we photograph our fourth re-enactment plaque
unveiled by a man carrying Ngatjumay genes
along with those of William Graham
the early stationmaster

we remember Eyre was near death
picture this tiny well saving him
oh no Graham's grandson says *I dug that hole
Eyre's wells are east and west of here*

they say at the western Wununda
you can still see the hoofmarks of his horses

on Baxter Cliffs

i
everything bites me

Lin's voice is matter-of-fact
her ankle red & swollen

we rally with years of advice
offers of instant cures

no blue bag or ammonia here
but from our small well-packed kits
come jars & tubes: betadine & gentian violet
stingose no-rash & comfrey ointment
praxyl animine & eurax
each with a personal guarantee

too many riches
Lin's unfamiliar predicament

ii
such stark existence on these cliffs
so little food & waterless

Eyre's only choice is
to advance or go back

alone of the five he will choose to go on
and his the choice that counts

Cootachah

he loves the boys   especially Cootachah
the youngest   now twelve

who most often rides beside him
as he checks the early routes

swimming with Eyre along the southern coast
his master walking so he may ride

excused the long watches of the night
given twice the meat ration Eyre and Baxter have

on the great cliffs when desperate for water
all but Eyre wish to return

Wylie & Neramberein are allowed to leave
Cootachah must stay

the boys

they didn't make it alone for long
after four days' hunger & with little water

the older boys return
& are forgiven   Wylie at least contrite

two days later on the cliffs
the surly Neramberein

persuades young Cootachah
to steal supplies with him & sneak away

when the despairing Baxter wakes
they shoot him in the chest and flee

only to follow Eyre and Wylie all the next day
crying like a native dog

for safety Eyre plans to shoot Neramberein
(never young Cootachah) but cannot

unarmed he tries to speak with them
hears words he will never forget

Oh massa, we don't want you, we want Wylie

Baxter's bones

i

no fixed abode
riding & walking behind Eyre & the stock
sleeping under canvas under stars
then a noise   a shot   a fall

& Baxter sleeps again under the stars

no soil for a grave
on that extensive limestone plate
Eyre wraps his *faithful follower*
in a blanket and leaves him
within *sound of the pinwing and the gull*

ii

forty years later the telegraph
has followed their walk

& Ngatjumay people tell the stationmaster
of bones on a cliff

the linesman returns with a skeleton
& relics of the camp but no head

where is your head John Baxter?

the bones are sewn into a calico bag
for the pony messenger to take to Perth

in Devon Eyre is pleased his friend
can now have Christian burial

not so fast Edward John
no burial has been recorded

the bones are in a government file
when a gunlock is added five years later

after a further forty-two years
the file and gunlock are discovered

but no bones

last week they were said
to be in Adelaide

is Baxter another Abraham
with no continuing city?

or does his spirit wander
until his bones are home?

Baxter's memorial

still hard to find — the track
weaves through scrub near Jindra waterhole
(so different a story if Eyre had known)

we are relieved to arrive
at *Australia's loneliest monument*
set in a Chagall tableau:

posies of white everlastings
bunch from brown earth
flowers in a vase floating over two lovers

a concrete pillar on the hard limestone crust
is too sharp-edged & square
for the surrounding twisted mallees

on the brass plate the overseer
has become EXPLORER & COMPANION
KILLED HERE BY THE NATIVES

fearing this might imply the nearby tribes
locals hasten to say the killers
came *from Sydney-side*

we rush to photograph the daisies
run over the bare ground
in search of the perfect shot

banksia

Those only who have looked out with the eagerness and anxiety of a person in my situation . . . can appreciate the degree of satisfaction with which I recognized and welcomed the first appearance of the Banksia.

real monkey's birthday weather
as Ilse & Claire set off to photograph
the acres of banksias
sweeping up dunes & along the track
afternoon light catching the raindrops
on leaves & flowers

Eyre's plant is a new species Ilse says:
Banksia epica   named for his epic journey

have you studied botany?
yes & biology   languages
Japanese the latest
I love to study

after the war when life depended
on a few peas in a lot of water
& a splash through the border at midnight
she arrived in Adelaide with no English
studied till 2 am for school & university
after work in the pub
& two kids to look after

I got my BA but stayed on cleaning
it's more secure than contract teaching
I bought a little rundown house
now all my money goes on that — and this

her hand includes the dunes
the distant hills
the banksia

west

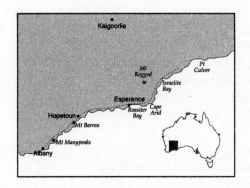

the cold

Now the winter had set in, and we were sadly unprepared to meet its inclemency, the cold at night became so intense as to occasion me agonies of pain; and the poor native was in the same predicament.

not only the cold:
they were faint & ill
and *suffered most excruciating pains*
after killing & eating the weakest horse

was the cold also in Eyre's spirit?

now past the danger of ambush and thirst
he brooded on the overseer's death
& the betrayal of the boys he loved
no longer fearful *of* but *for* them

two brown birds peer out to sea
Eyre & Wylie we call them

something defeated about them
for heroes

Israelite Bay

i

sailing over Wylie Scarp
into a sea of dismal heath

it is easy to believe in a flat earth
and a drop into space

until we see chimneys
like palm trees on the horizon

& arrive at last to discover
few human imprints

if you except a weightlifting machine
beside the road

the grandiose Telegraph Station ruins
with three gaping slits for non-existent mail

two occasional fishermen's camps
five graves

& the sole resident who lives with his TV
near the rubble of Glencoe homestead

the jetty once busy with sheep fish & mica
begins fifty metres out from land

and the fig tree across the lake — all that remains
of the first station — bears very small figs

ii

we heard at least three origins
of the Bay's surprising name:

first   a Dutch sailor was put ashore
giving fair hair & long noses
to his descendants who explorers thought
must be the lost tribe of Israel

then   the border with uncircumcised tribes
is just to the south & explorers noticed
the natives practise here
the Israelitish custom

thirdly   in the 1860s
when men rowed wool to ships standing off
a nervous captain Abrahamson
anchored out so far
the rowing was hard & dangerous

they named the Bay
for the Israelite who never entered it

day off

*we had neither spirit nor energy left . . . I felt, on such occasions, that
I could have sat quietly and contentedly, and let the glass of life glide
away to its last sand.*

after weeks of bumpy tracks
ecstasy is a day without travel

the trailer has done a bearing
& we are delighted to be
turned loose among wildflowers
while the men fix things or fail to

the trailer must be left under Mt Ragged
we make a beach camp
under a gibbous moon
with clouds becoming caves   a unicorn   fish

we walk miles over white sand
in a blue morning
watch sea eagles & pied oystercatchers

Ilse collects shells   inspects bird tracks
the hardy ones swim in clear water
cold from the south

Lin floats on her back musing
how lucky we are — the best climate
the best wildflowers
the best country

yes (Claire's tone just a touch acerbic)
and best to be white & middleclass

a rip develops

with hearts pounding
we heave ourselves to shore

Point Malcolm

on the outer side the waves were breaking with frightful violence . . .
I was very nearly terminating my crab hunting and expedition at
the same time.

i
that narrow point of glittering rocks
divides calm from wild

swirls like the annual rings
of pine trees

black   white   orange & gold
transform the shattered boulders

Lin's fluorescent bootlaces are outshone
by mica-flecks dancing in the sun

weathering is not enough:
rocks must be broken to shine

ii
thirty years
after Eyre Wylie & the horses

were restored by *six clear days*
at this most favourable position

a barn was first built on the sheltered side
then a kitchen & bedroom

and a surreal letterbox on its tall post
at the edge of a wide & empty beach

a lantern placed on top to guide the rowboat in
snuffed out by the departing sailors

I have seen a painting of that letterbox
and want to believe the story

but who would come & go at night?
why not wait for morning & a cup of tea?

the well & homestead are ruins now
a whalebone bleaching on the grass

a petrified tree wedged against the point
and the mountain Eyre saw as Ragged

(Paringunya to the Ngatjumay)
lifts fairy towers on our horizon

Cape Arid

the island floats as magic islands must
peaks & towers

and Webb's old goatskin hermit
an exhausted woman of a mountain

toughened & worn by southern wind & rain
lies silent now   relaxed

a line of mist holds her above the playful sea
God's only message for today: enjoy

last night we arrived late
the Variety Club Bash already in camp:

dismembered plastic women protruding from cars
busts & legs & brightly striped fire-engines

streamers & drunk men everywhere
Hey Ron here's a busload of women wanting sex

the guy opened the door   saw eight tired grey heads
& said *they look alright*

bring condoms alcohol & drugs tonight
we smiled as mothers do when children are outrageous

they do it for charity Elsie said
                              as Jim drove us to a quieter camp

Rossiter Bay

at last [we] were delighted beyond measure to perceive to the westward
the masts of a large ship . . .

the re-enactment walkers made it on time
the townsfolk came in crowds

a hundred and fifty years to the day
after the ship's captain met the exhausted pair

the yacht *Sixpak* brought *Captain Rossiter* ashore
a farmer lent horses for *Wylie & Eyre*

permits approved their signal fire
if it was in a drum

a fine picnic day with barbecues
matched *the good cheer set before us*

on board the hospitable Mississippi
where a little brandy made Eyre tipsy

in contrast to that earlier day
tragedy came at the end:

the horses led into their truck
(the bolts not properly home)

were flung onto the winding road
to die where Eyre was saved

Lucky Bay

in violent seas Flinders risked disaster
to steer for the coast
finding at dusk this bay

from the shelter of his cabin
Eyre *heard the wind roar*
and the rain drive with unusual wildness

for us
wide rainbow over storm-tossed islands
in the Archipelago of the Recherche

misty rain on monster rocks:
druids at prayer on the hillside
white horses in a wild sea

       & hot water in the campground

south coast

i

Every thing that I wished for, was given to me
flour biscuits rice beef pork sugar tea butter & brandy

the Captain's final gift
six bottles of wine, and a tin of sardines

after twelve days' respite on board
they now expect to reach their goal

too much water their foremost problem
& a fire burning their new warm clothes

ii

Eyre was not the first white man
to trudge these swampy flats:

five years earlier two shipwrecked youths
were put ashore by Black Jack Anderson

with no gunpowder   no supplies   no rescuing ship
living on limpets roots & crabs

Newell & Manning reached Albany
with no acclaim

forbidden

following Eyre's route along this coast
we come to a locked gate
and a sign:

XANADU
NO THROUGH ROAD
NO BEACH ACCESS

Lorna complains
these legendary kingdoms
seldom invite us to their pleasure-domes

whether of hash or honey-dew

Esperance

first stores for weeks
we scatter for films & coffee
return with arms full of parcels:

presents for children
grandchildren   nephews' children
friends' children

presents to tell children they are special
that nothing is demanded
they don't have to come top
make the team   clean up their rooms

I remember my aunts
& the postcards from Tonga
the books   the model of St Paul's

the silver mug with my name engraved
the huge boxed Easter eggs
from an aunt not family but friend

I remember my children's aunts
& the clothes I didn't have to sew
the books I didn't have to buy

keep on singing it Judy Small
sing for maiden aunts & add grannies
who delight in the riches of giving

Wylie's progress

already on monuments
as we go westward
he makes it to the maps

first a scarp that no-one visits
then he scores a Head and Bay
outside Esperance city of hope

no landmark for him
in hometown Albany
save for a couple of plaques

though Eyre arranged
for a permanent allowance
of flour & tobacco   sent him a gun

he lost a Government post
(too many relatives the official said)
soon disappears from the Sound

except on the first post
of the old telegraph line where a new
plaque to Wylie balances one for Eyre

& for the first time we read
the survival of the two men was largely due
to their dependence on each other

markers

i
at Pink Lakes the re-enactment plaque
has gone   taken for scrap
or by some collector of epic journeys?

ii
we drive down country tracks
can find no trace of the river
named for Eyre

though the crossroads monument
at the farm gate looks very sure
Eyre came this way

iii
the Hopetoun memorial
divided the town:
now on the beacon guiding ships

some people are certain it should be
under the ledge on East Mt Barren
where Eyre & Wylie slept

iv
a local man believes the J and F
carved into a tree are not John Forrest's
but the surviving parts of E J E

he is so insistent
his sons won't speak to him

hakea

if Ilse asks for one more photo stop
I'll scream

bumpy tracks have stiffened Helen's back
she wants a cup of tea

we pass a stretch of bush alight
with royal hakea: autumn in spring

their brilliant reds & golds enabling them
to live in arid places

(such functional splendour
must be another sign of grace)

Ilse asks Jim to stop
Helen grabs her camera   is next out of the bus

the Barrens

Most properly had it been called Mount Barren, for a more wretched
arid-looking country never existed . . .

on the campground grass above the waters
Claire Lin & Lorna are dancing
(so romantic those blue peaks across the bay)

they try to remember the old steps:
Tangoette   the Modern Waltz   Pride of Erin

Helen shakes her head
        you've got it wrong   step sideways
        — come on Helen show us how
        no
        — come on   please
        NO   try it again yourselves

in her sleeping bag that night
Claire remembers Helen's first conversation:
        my husband just died   took a year to do
        hit by a car after our dancing class
        you'd think he'd be fit enough to jump clear

next morning Claire joins Helen at the lookout
        I'm sorry I was thoughtless last night
        forgetting your loss
        dancing the last thing you'd want to do

        that's alright   all part of the cure
        it's why I came

the collector

Beauty is walled in freedom
                              Francis Webb

I lift the Pentax to catch
Ilse on the beach
collecting shells

ever since she dashed
through a stream
to cross the Wall
she collects things

the three Mt Barrens
fifty kilometres apart
are the background

but I must move
to crop the foreground
include a cliff

I who have never known hunger
am also a collector

whinger

Eyre was a bit of a whinger
so one of the re-enactment walkers
is supposed to have said
to the support group bringing beer
towards the end
of their fifteen-hundred-kilometre trek

she hadn't found the scrub so tough
only one really hot day & three of rain

Mt Manypeaks

Lorna at the mountain
thinks of sex
so many curls & slips
astonishing high places
crests to slide over

so bountiful
the country below
where Eyre squelched
through mud

after the desert
too much rain

Lorna finds
she has a thirst

Albany

a swamp when Eyre arrived
now manicured grass

an exercise course   reedy lakes
and notices:

NO ACCESS
DOGS MUST BE ON A LEASH

POTENTIAL WATER HAZARD
CHILDREN MUST BE SUPERVISED

if Eyre had obeyed *his* orders
we wouldn't now be strolling in this Eyre Park

cures

what's next Lin —
signing up for another trip?

some tests first Helen   I had a mastectomy
earlier this year & a bit of chemo

of course! Helen recognizes now
(so late) those wispy curls

contemplates her year — and Lin's:
the cure is working

journey's end

the rain was falling in torrents
a thousand reflections crowded my mind
we had long been given up as lost

the *wild joyous cry* of Wylie's welcome
the *wordless weeping pleasure* of his family
contrast with Eyre's solitary walk to Sherratt's hotel
& the comfort of brandy

he had lost everything except the British flag —
and that he carried back to Adelaide
pure and unsullied
as his own stainless character

within a week Eyre embarks on the *Truelove*
& dozens of Wylie's people beg to go with him

ii 1991

they walk in rain with hundreds of residents
past the two huge pines Eyre is said to have planted

Governor and Mayor greet them at Albany Town Hall
with speeches & afternoon tea

the letter   the crock of wine   the soil are handed over
& the flag   like the one Eyre refused to leave

and the three who have together
re-enacted his walk

carry away a few seeds
& part without planning to meet

iii 1993

so Rob Royish under its granite mountains
the town is veiled in mist
the woman serving coffee says
on days like this
she runs down York Street to the harbour
to cry for her faraway Loch Earn

the mist turns to isolating rain
we're glad to be in cabins
this last night & a special chicken dinner —
Jim's been a good cook

too wet for a final walk to the beach
we sit in the largest room drinking
Jim is worried about our damaged trailer
Tom & Claude are drunk & talkative

Meg & Elsie laugh at their stories
Lorna goes out to ring her friend
the rest of us smile & look at our watches
as some rare fabric dissolves

iv

one night on the cliffs beyond Twilight Cove
Claire recalled a Canadian film
where elderly women on a stranded bus
bit by bit unveiled their lives

that's us Claire
women travelling alone together
for a time

envoi

Si Je Puis

Si Je Puis ever has been, and still is, my first resolve . . .

if I can
    Australia is better than the army
if I can
    farming is better than employment
if I can
    overlanding is better than farming
if I can
    exploration is better than overlanding
if I can
    I wish a more honourable and disinterested
    distinction than by money
if I can
    I want to find the still unknown and mysterious
    centre of this vast continent
if I can
    I will have a reputation I shall be proud of

veteran

outside his neat suburban bungalow
I asked the eighty-year-old
for the highlight of his thousand-mile walk

he pointed to a vigorous young eucalypt
(*E. tetragona*)
with a blush on its blue-grey foliage

I saw one near Cape Arid
with moonlight
striking the dew on its leaves

I brought seed back
and planted one where the street light
will make it shine

for Eyre? I asked
for me

letter

Dear Miriel

Your letter followed me
of course you may use
the story of my husband's death

I tried to read my sister your poem
but it stuck in my throat
time takes its time

the soil is awful here
I have started a garden
& am planting trees

I always wanted to be called Helen

Notes

Quotations from Eyre, in *Garamond Italic* in this text, are taken mostly from his *Journals of Expeditions of Discovery into Central Australia, and Overland from Adelaide to King George's Sound, in the years 1840–1* (vols 1 & 2, London, T. and W. Boone, 1845), but also from *Edward Eyre's Autobiographical Narrative 1832–1839* (ed. Jill Waterhouse, London, Caliban Books, 1984) and from various letters held in the Mitchell Library, the National Library of Australia and the State Library of South Australia. I have omitted words and phrases in places without, I hope, altering the sense of the passage.

departure. Eyre's first exploring expedition from Adelaide, from 1 May to 29 June 1839, went north to Mt Arden depot, on to Mt Eyre (named later), and back through good land in the Clare valley and east, along the Murray, to Lake Alexandrina and so to Adelaide. A second in 1839 explored Eyre Peninsula, from Port Lincoln past Streaky Bay to Point Bell, across to Mt Arden and back. Another trip in early 1840 took sheep by boat to Albany and then overlanded them to York.

the Irish overseer. It is not absolutely certain but extremely likely that Baxter was the farm bailiff mentioned in Eyre's *Narrative*.

Mt Sturt. *Sturt: The Chipped Idol* is the title of Edgar Beale's study of Charles Sturt (Sydney University Press, 1979). Eyre met his mentor Sturt in Sydney in January 1837.

Sturt's desert pea. This species has now been reclassified as *Swainsona formosa*, honouring an 18th-century Englishman. I prefer to think of it as *Clianthus*, the glory flower!

fool's mate. Daisy Bates records, in *The Native Tribes of Western Australia* (ed. Isobel White, NLA, Canberra, 1985), that 'even along the edges of the great Nullarbor Plain there are springs, soaks and watering places which had Eyre but known, there would have been no tale to tell of tragedy and thirst'.

insufficient evidence. The sites of Eyre's wells are a source of much conjecture. At Fowlers Bay dunes may have covered the site.

misunderstanding. Eyre uses *road* in the earlier sense of a route or course.

death. Callan Park is a Sydney psychiatric hospital.

Wilson Bluff. Originally Kaldilyarra, the Bluff was named by Delisser, supposedly for 'Professor Wilson, the acclimatizer', but neither of the Wilsons who were 'acclimatizers' was a professor. The story is in R. Cockburn, *What's in a Name?: The Nomenclature of South Australia* (Adelaide, Ferguson Publications, 1984).

Eucla. Another version of the name is given by Daisy Bates, where it is the ancient track down the escarpment.

Mundrabilla. The early history of Mundrabilla, or Mondra Bellae, is in Peter Gifford, 'Murder and "The Execution of the Law" on the Nullarbor', in *Aboriginal History* (vol.18, 1994).

Cootachah. Cootachah and another little boy, Joshuing, left Mr Yalbone's party to join Eyre in June 1837. Joshuing 'defected' in 1838 with a group of dissatisfied workers whom Eyre called mutineers. Eyre often had Aboriginal boys with him. When he left Australia in 1845, he took two of them to England to educate at his expense. One was sent back to Australia, the other died aged seventeen.

the boys. *Crying like a native dog*: the words are Wylie's.

Baxter's bones. *Pinwing* is an old name for the penguin. The quote is from John Graham, the youth who, with the linesman Healy, found the site of Baxter's murder.

Cape Arid. The references are to Francis Webb's poem, 'Eyre All Alone'.

journey's end (i). The quote is from an account, supposedly by a relative, in the Mitchell Library. The flag was a centrepiece at the Adelaide dinner celebrating Eyre's return which the *Adelaide Independent* thought should have been cheaper, so that 'the better behaved classes might have checked those disgraceful exhibitions of magisterial outrage which blackened the evening from the moment His Excellency and the Chairman left'. We are not told when Eyre left. Captain Sturt was in the Chair.

Si Je Puis (*If I Can*). Eyre's family crest includes a sawn-off leg, supposedly suffered at Agincourt or Hastings, a broken knife and a faun. He was extremely proud of his ancient lineage, and used the image of an amputated leg on his visiting card.